It was October 21st, Anthony's birthday and race day in Franklin Square. Anthony, Alexis, Christal and Gabriella were sitting in the stands watching the cars speed round the track. A sleek red car roared into the lead. Anthony thought of Lightning McQueen from his favorite movie, *Cars*. He daydreamed that he was a car reporter at the Los Angeles International Speedway. The big race was over, and McQueen was at the Rust-eze tent with his friends and the press. As a reporter, Anthony had been sent to Los Angeles by his local newspaper to interview the famous Lightning McQueen! Alexis, Christal and Gabriella were also there, as car photographers.

Anthony wandered over to McQueen. 'This has been an amazing week for you, McQueen. Tell us how it all began.'

McQueen reflected on the week. 'Well, it all started a week ago at the Dinoco 400, the last race of the season. I admit I was pretty cocky and I thought the race was mine! It would be tough though! I was a rookie, racing against The King, the legend! And, of course, there was Chick. We were all tied for the season leading into the race. Whoever won, would win the season title and the Piston Cup which I'd been dreaming about my whole life.

'It was also The King's last race which meant his Dinoco sponsorship was up for grabs. I really wanted to be sponsored by Dinoco. But so did Chick and he would do anything to win.

'Anthony, the race was wild! Chick slammed into me and I skidded off the track, but I managed to regain control. Then as everyone pulled into the pit, I took the lead. When I had to refuel I thought I'd save time and I ignored my team's advice to change my tires. In the final lap, my rear tires blew! The King and Chick caught up to me. We crossed the finish line together. It was a three-way tie, and there would be a tie-breaker race a week later in California. I had to get there first and wanted to leave right away. But Mack, my driver, reminded me that I had to check in with my sponsors, Rust-eze.

DINOCO

DINOCO

43   43   43

"Okay, Okay,' I thought. I didn't want to, but I went to the Rust-eze tent. I hated that place back then. I thought I was gonna be the next great champ. I wanted a bigger, better sponsor—one that would bring me fame, fortune—all the perks of being a superstar. I wanted Dinoco, not a company that made rust ointment!'

'Have you ever interviewed a rusty car, Anthony? There was this one car whose rusty bumper kept falling off every time he talked! I didn't want to spend one more minute with the Rust-eze fans. Yeah, I know, I had a lot to learn!

'Anyway, when we finally were ready to go, I got settled inside Mack's trailer for the long drive to California.

'Let me tell you, Anthony,' said McQueen, 'that was the beginning of a whole new adventure.

'It was a long trip and I couldn't keep my eyes open,' recalled McQueen. 'Still I kept pushing poor Mack so we could get there first. But Mack ended up falling asleep. Totally my fault. The next thing I knew, I woke up in the middle of oncoming traffic. That was scary. You know my headlights are just stickers so I couldn't see a thing. I saw some lights on the horizon, and, thinking it was Mack, I sped off in that direction.

'Then I heard a siren behind me. An old police cruiser was in hot pursuit! Poor Sheriff was racing so hard to catch me that his muffler practically cracked open. I heard a loud bang, and, well, I must admit, I thought I was being shot at!

'Suddenly I found myself racing through this sleepy little town called Radiator Springs, Anthony. I crashed into a fence and lost control. Then I wreaked havoc on the town road and ended upside down hanging from a telephone pole. Next thing I knew I woke up inside the impound lot.'

'Is that where you met Mater, the tow truck?' asked Anthony.

'That's right,' replied McQueen. 'Little did I know that rusty truck would become my best friend. I tried to trick him into setting me free, but Sheriff turned up.

'Sheriff told Mater to take me to traffic court. I thought I'd be off the hook and out of town in no time. I was a famous race car! Unfortunately, the townsfolk didn't know who I was. They hated me for messing up their town. I did make a pretty big mess of things.

'The judge, Doc Hudson was ready to let me go but more trouble was brewing.

'Just then, a beautiful sports car named Sally drove in. It turned out she was the town attorney and she had other ideas. She convinced Doc to make me fix the road!'

'How could they make a famous racing car fix the road?' asked Anthony.

'I had no choice,' replied McQueen. 'They hooked me to Bessie, the road-paving machine. I had to get out of there. The race was only days away. So I dragged Bessie around for about an hour until I finished the road. It was sloppy, but I didn't think it was any worse than the rest of the town. But the townsfolk weren't happy. Doc told me to scrape it off and start over again. He was really angry.

'Then Doc gave me the surprise of my life.
He challenged me to a race. The deal was
that if I won, I could leave Radiator Springs.
If he won, I would have to do the road again.'

'That should have been easy for you, McQueen,' said Anthony.

'Well, I thought so!' replied McQueen.

'I roared off before Doc could even start his engine. I wanted to show those townsfolk how fast a real race car could go. But, I got another lesson and this time it really hurt. I took a sharp left turn, spun out right, and dropped over a ledge into a patch of cactus!

'A deal was a deal and I had to go back to work on the road,' said McQueen. 'This time, I was determined to get it right. I had to get out of there; and after Doc had humiliated me, I was determined to prove myself. I worked hard all night. When the town cars awoke, even they were impressed with the new stretch of road. They even seemed to want to fix up their shops. Radiator Springs was beginning to look good.'

'So you could leave town then?' asked Anthony.

'I wasn't quite finished. I ran out of tar. I asked Sheriff to take me to the dirt track to practice the turn that had wiped me out,' replied McQueen. 'But I just couldn't get it.

'That's when I saw Doc watching. 'This is dirt,' he told me. 'You gotta turn right to go left.' I thought he was crazy. Still, I gave it a try… and wiped out again.

'The next morning, I went to find Sheriff to get my fuel ration. He was at Doc's clinic, and Doc shooed me away.

'I wandered in to Doc's back garage and you'll never guess what I found—a Piston Cup inscribed with the name 'Hudson Hornet'. Doc was a racing champion, the Fabulous Hudson Hornet! Just then Doc appeared in the doorway. He was furious that I'd been snooping around. He pushed me out. I raced to tell everyone at Flo's, but they didn't believe me!

'Later, Sally invited me for a drive up the mountain. You know, I was full of fuel and could have just taken off, but something kept me there. The view was beautiful, and so was Sally! She told me about how she came to Radiator Springs and what a busy town it was before the Interstate went through. It really made me think about that place and the folks who lived there.'

The Daily Exhaust

EXTRA FINAL

CRASH!
HUDSON HORNET OUT FOR SEASON

Season Ender Fender Bender
Puts Young Hornet in Garage

'Did you end up talking to Doc again?' asked Anthony.

'Well, I actually caught him racing out at the track. He was amazing! I followed him back to his office. I asked him why he quit racing when he was at the top,' replied McQueen.

'Doc showed me a newspaper article about a huge wreck he'd been in. When he got fixed up and returned to the racing world, they told him he had been replaced by a rookie. That's why he hated me so much, I guess. I told him I wasn't like that, but then he asked me when the last time was that I cared for anything but myself. I was speechless. Doc told me to finish the road and leave town. I worked all night. The next morning, the road was done.'

'So why didn't you leave town right away?' asked Anthony.

'I wanted to help my new friends. I went shopping at every store in town. And I even arranged for a little surprise for Sally. I got all of the townsfolk to fix their neon signs. On my cue, the whole town lit up.'

'You must have felt so proud, McQueen! I wish I'd been there to see it,' said Anthony.

'Yeah. It was pretty much... fantastic,' replied McQueen. 'Everyone started cruising the streets. Of course, I tried to pair up with Sally, but the other cars kept separating us! Radiator Springs had come alive again and the townsfolk loved it. It was really nice to slow down you know.

'Then everything got crazy, Anthony. One minute I was cruising with Sally, and the next, Radiator Springs was crawling with media. I was swamped with questions about where I'd been and was I still going to race for the Piston Cup.

'Come to think of it, though, I didn't see you there, Anthony, or Alexis or Christal or Gabriella.

'Harv, my agent, started talking to me over Mack's speakerphone (thank goodness Mack was there). Harv said I had to get to California quickly or Dinoco was history.

'I found Sally, but I didn't know what to say. Sally wished me good luck and disappeared in the crowd. Before I knew it I was leaving Radiator Springs behind.'

'Leaving must have made you very sad, but you had to think of your career didn't you?' asked Anthony.

'Honestly, I really wasn't thinking that much about my career. I had grown to love Radiator Springs, it had become almost like home to me,' replied McQueen.

'You didn't even get to say goodbye to Mater, did you?' asked Anthony.

'No, I didn't even get to say goodbye to my new best friend,' replied McQueen. 'That crazy tow truck. I didn't know how to be a friend until I met him. He taught me lots of stuff—even how to drive backwards.

'Then today, I found myself in the middle of the biggest race of my life, and all I could think of was Radiator Springs. Winning just didn't seem important without my friends. Not only was I losing the race, but I almost crashed into a wall.

'Then the most amazing thing happened. I heard Doc over the radio! He was saying how he hadn't come all this way to see me quit! I looked over to my pit and there was the whole crew from Radiator Springs. They had all come to support me! It was the best feeling. I started really racing again. I used the backwards driving trick Mater had taught me, and I used the 'turn right to go left' secret Doc had taught me. Soon enough I found myself in the lead, thanks to my friends.

'Just then I heard the crowd gasp. I looked in the big screen. Chick had rammed The King causing a huge crash. It was terrible! This was The King! He rolled and crashed in a heap.

'I'm telling you, I almost heard Doc's voice in my head as I remembered how he had crashed and been kicked out of the racing world for good. So I stopped. Yup, I stopped right before the finish line, and Chick raced past to win the race. I didn't care. I had only one thing on my mind—I had to help The King finish his last race. I reversed and pushed The King over the finish line. I guess you could say the crowd kind of went wild. I knew I had done the right thing. As for Chick? Well, you saw it—he was booed off the stage when he got his trophy.'

'You did an incredible thing!' Anthony remarked.

'Well, I've learned a lot about a lot of things this week, Anthony,' replied McQueen. 'Mostly I learned about friendship and caring about others. Life's about taking the time to enjoy the journey—not just getting to the finish line first.'

McQueen had to finish his interview then and he thanked Anthony before he drove off to meet his friends.

McQueen was offered the Dinoco sponsorship and, although he was flattered, he turned down the offer as he'd decided to stay loyal to the Rust-eze gang. He did ask Tex, Dinoco's owner, for one small thing. He'd promised his best friend, Mater, a ride in a helicopter!

McQueen returned to Radiator Springs where he set up his racing headquarters. He had everything he needed—friends, a great team, Doc as his crew chief, and, of course, Sally.

Why would he go anywhere else?

This personalized Disney • PIXAR Cars book was especially created for Anthony Hoda of 703 Eileen Court, Franklin Square, with love from Aunt Casey & Uncle Kevin.

If you ordered multiple books, they may be mailed separately — please allow a few days for differences in delivery times.

0782 000033 0001 01 DS 0001

0782000033000101